COBRA CONSIGNMENT

Sarah Dixon

Illustrated by Ann Johns

Contents

About this Book

Cobra Consignment is a thrilling adventure story, packed with fiendish puzzles which must be solved to unravel the plot. If you get stuck – and you may – there are clues on page 42 to point you in the right direction. You will find all the answers at the back of the book. If you don't need to look at these, you may be a genius.

Off to Magnos

As the hot, airless bus hurtled along the road to the port, Nat pulled out a crumpled letter. It had only arrived a week ago and he had read it countless times since then. Cousin Al, the famous archeologist, had invited him to the island of Magnos to help on his latest dig. It sounded too good to be true – two weeks of sun, sea and ancient treasure! There had to be a catch somewhere …

Villa Magnotaur
Magnotaur Passage
Town Wall
Magnos Town

Dear Nat,
How do you like the sound of two weeks on the sunny island of Magnos? The ex-film star, Strega Nimbus (remember Battlestar Elektra?) has organized a new excavation of the ancient city above Magnos Town. She's convinced that its ruins hold the key to the whereabouts of the legendary treasure of Magnos, the so-called Cobra Gold. I'm in charge of the dig and I desperately need more help. So far there's only me, my assistant, Lina, and, occasionally, Strega herself!

It's easy to get here. There are two ferries a day which leave the port of Kaos at 5am and 7pm. The crossing takes about four hours. If you come over next week, you'll arrive in time for the Festival of the Magnotaur, which - I'm told - is not to be missed!

Look forward to seeing you!

Al

Here is the news at 6:30. This afternoon thieves stole the priceless Pipes of Paxi from Kaos Museum. The discovery of a red snake earring at the scene of the crime has led police to link the theft with the notorious gangsters and masters of disguise, Niagara Smith and Bronson Colt …

Strega and Lina on site - at lunch

Me outside Villa Magnotaur

3

Distress at Sea

The bus shuddered to a halt at the port. Nat grabbed his heavy backpack and stumbled out. He glanced at his watch and gulped. It was nearly seven o'clock – the Magnos ferry was due to leave any minute.

Nat dodged past a small dog and a man in a suit carrying armfuls of documents, and hurried down the dock to the ferry.

Suddenly Nat heard a shout. He turned to see the man in the suit wave at a boat. One of his documents lay flapping in the breeze behind him.

Nat dashed over and retrieved it. Close up, it looked just like an ordinary pink notebook – except for the writing on the cover. After an anxious glance at the ferry, he raced after the man.

The man was with two strange characters in funny white smocks and hats. They were deep in conversation and didn't notice Nat approach.

"Bad news from Hood," the man rasped. "The final cobra consignment has been held up in Enchillada. Take this lot straight to base. We'll keep Lamia informed about the movements of the …"

Nat cleared his throat. The man spun around and glared at him. Then he saw what was in Nat's hand.

"I'll take that!" he snapped. "Now push off, or else …"

His words were drowned by the blast of a ship's hooter. Nat looked up, horrorstruck. He was about to miss the ferry.

Three hours later, Nat wished he HAD missed the ferry. The boat heaved up and down as huge waves smashed against its sides. Lightning flashed overhead while passengers cowered miserably below deck.

The storm raged on and on. Was there any chance that the ferry was near Magnos? Nat struggled up onto the deck and stared out across the tossing sea, looking for signs of land.

A feeble light flickered ahead. He blinked as the light flashed again ... and again. A distress signal!

The signal was obviously in Morse code. Quickly, Nat pulled out his notebook and jotted down the sequence of short and long flashes, using dots and dashes.

After the final flash, Nat desperately tried to decipher his scribbles. If only he could remember all of the Morse alphabet – not that it would be much help. The signal seemed to be in a foreign language ...

Then it came to Nat in a flash. Of course! The message sent in Morse code must be in another code.

What does it say?

5

Ransacked!

Half an hour later, the storm vanished and the ferry chugged into the calm waters of Magnos port.

While Nat wandered up and down the waterfront, looking for Al, the Morse message whirred around in his head. It hadn't been a distress signal after all. But why had it been sent the wrong way around? And why did the name Lamia ring a faint bell?

Nat glanced anxiously at his watch. Another half hour had gone by and there was still no sign of Al. What had happened to him? Surely he hadn't forgotten that Nat was coming.

Shivering in the chilly night air, Nat decided to find his own way to Al's house, Villa Magnotaur. He checked the address on Al's letter, then headed up the steep hill into the town.

An hour and 57 wrong turns later, Nat stumbled down the steps from the top of the town wall, feeling very lost. As he scanned the rooftops, he spotted a tiny house with red tiles, half hidden by vines. He had found Villa Magnotaur at last!

Nat hurried down to the dimly lit street, raced through an arch and ran up a short flight of steps to the villa.

The door hung open … but once inside, Nat looked around in disbelief. The place had been ransacked. The contents of every cupboard and drawer had been tipped out, and Al was nowhere to be seen. Where was he? What was going on?

Among the debris, Nat caught sight of a symbol on a typed note. Where had he seen it before?

September 1

NEWS IN BRIEF
SERPENT'S EYE REWARD

The Geological Society of the Republic of Enchillada is offering a reward of $1,000 for information leading to the recovery of the Serpent's Eye. This priceless crystal of venomite was stolen from the society's headquarters in Enchillada City last month.

MISSING PROF SPOTTED

Missing scientist Professor Una Eco has been spotted in Kaos City. The world-famous inventor disappeared from her lab in Hudlum City three months ago. Detectives have confirmed that her disappearance is not linked with the recent activities of the notorious Syndicate gang.

ATTN TAKI
HOTEL CERBERUS
STYX STREET

Sept 14

Rendezvous with S and C at 01:11 at Hotel Digitalis. First collect cargo from Villa Magnotaur at 22:30. To reach VM, turn L at T junction at end of Styx St, go straight on at X roads, then turn R at end of road. VM is at end of passage on R. Load cargo then take L fork to X roads. Turn L and follow road to T junction. Turn L and go to second hotel on L (Hotel Hydra). Leave HH at 00:30 and turn left, then L again and go across X roads to T junction. Turn R, then L at X roads. At end of road, turn L. As you drive on, you'll see HD straight ahead.
NB PICK UP KAOS TODAY FROM VM

MAGNOS TOWN

to Mt Ophis

to the Ancient City

Key

- ▬ Passage (pedestrians only)
- 🚢 Ferry
- ● Hotel
- Town Wall
- arch tower steps
- ① Museum
- ② Old Palace
- ③ Town Hall
- ④ Castle
- ⑤ Paxi Square

to Toros village

to Thebe's cave

arrival (base) June 21
consignment arrival (kaos) June 26 June 20 July 1 June 24 June 30
pipes cylinders

The note was addressed to someone called Taki. It contained a long list of directions to a rendezvous at Hotel Digitalis at eleven minutes past one, an odd time for a meeting … yet strangely familiar.

The note seemed to be Nat's only lead. He decided to go to the rendezvous. If Al wasn't there, Taki might know where he was.

Nat checked his watch. It was almost one o'clock. How would he ever reach the rendezvous in time? There had to be a short cut.

Luckily, a map of Magnos Town was lying on the floor, but none of the streets or hotels was named.

Where is Hotel Digitalis?
What is Nat's short cut?

7

Familiar Faces

A distant clock struck one as Nat shut the door and quickly slipped a note underneath, just in case Al turned up.

The short cut took much longer than Nat expected. Half an hour later, he had nearly reached Hotel Digitalis when he stopped dead. There were muffled voices ahead and they didn't sound friendly.

Nat hastily scrambled up a crumbling wall and stared at the strange scene in front of him.

A battered truck was parked outside the hotel, next to a boat. A sailor busily cleared the deck, while two familiar looking characters in white lowered the tailgate of the truck. All three were listening to a cloaked woman just below Nat.

"Hurry up and load the cargo," the woman snapped. "Once that's done Taki, go back to Villa Magnotaur and find that magazine. And don't mess up this time!"

"Meanwhile, Bron," she continued, "you must go straight to the meeting. The Medusa will return later to pick up the final consignment. Bogartus will fill you in with the details."

Nat watched the duo in white lug an enormous carpet out of the truck. Groaning under its weight, they staggered over to the boat. Just as they lowered their burden onto the deck, Nat glimpsed something hidden in its folds.

He leaned forward to take a closer look, missed his footing and crashed into a tangle of spiky bushes below.

The duo instantly dropped the carpet and dashed over to the wall, armed with flashlights.

"Hands up!" barked a woman. To Nat's surprise, the voice belonged to one of the characters in white. He crouched among the prickly leaves, not daring to move until she finally disappeared into the shadows.

Nat carefully extricated himself from his hiding place and darted over to a gateway, only to spot the sailor lurking under the arch.

In desperation he clambered up onto the wall. Suddenly he heard a shout behind him.

Quickly, he jumped down to the road, raced over to the truck and dived under a sheet of tarpaulin.

OUCH! Something sharp jabbed into Nat's hand. He held the object up to the glow from the rear light.

It was a snake shaped earring. Something about it jogged Nat's memory. He gasped in disbelief as it slowly dawned on him who the strange duo in white really were. So much for the masters of disguise!

Who are they?

To the Ancient City

Hurry up, or you'll miss the meeting.

Heavy footsteps stomped up to the truck. Trapped under the tarpaulin in the back, Nat held his breath as someone climbed into the cab. The engine wheezed uncertainly then roared to life. The truck lurched forward, then veered left up a steep, dusty track.

As the truck raced through the darkness, Nat tried to make sense of his latest discovery. Unlikely as it might seem, the couple in white were none other than the notorious gangsters, Niagara Smith and Bronson Colt! The duo were implicated in a theft from Kaos Museum. But what were they doing on Magnos ... and where was Al?

The truck bounded over a series of potholes then squealed to a halt. Nat peered out from under the tarpaulin and watched the bizarrely dressed figure of Bronson Colt clamber out, stare at a scrap of yellow paper, then scurry through an arch in a high wall. No one else was around, so Nat slipped out and tiptoed after him.

Hidden in the shadows, Nat followed the gangster down a long flight of steps and up some stairs to a balcony. Then the trail ran cold ...

MEHEHE! A goat was nibbling at Bronson's scrap of paper. Nat hastily rescued the fragment. He scanned its contents, then darted over to the edge of the balcony. The moonlight shone on the ruins of an ancient city below. This must be the site of Al's dig – and one of the ruined buildings was Bronson's mystery destination.

Which one?

Meeting at Treasury 2:30 am Sept 15

THE ANCIENT CITY OF MAGNOS
East Quarter ***

Well worth seeing! Five buildings (marked A, B, C, D and E on the plan) are particularly worthy of note. Each is the work of one of the five famous architects of Ancient Kaos – Vikarios, Prekarios, Spurios, Tritos and Notalos (see page 4).

The **Gymnasium** should be seen before A and D. This is where the muscle-bound athletes of Ancient Magnos perfected their amazing triple back somersaults.

The **Amphitheater** (B) is still in use to this day. Together with E, it has been wrongly attributed to Vikarios, then to his arch rival, Tritos, and later to Spurios, the builder of C.

The **House of Althea**, beyond D, was once decorated with fine frescoes, now on display in Magnos Museum.

The **Temple of Paxi** was built by Prekarios. It honors the god Paxi, whose pipes were brought to Magnos by the Magnotaur.

The **Treasury** has been wrongly attributed to Spurios, Vikarios and Notalos. It was said to house the legendary treasures of Magnos, which the islanders sent as tribute to the Cobras of Cobradiki (see page 6 for a full account of the Cobra legend).

11

A Bizarre Meeting

Clutching Bronson's scrap of paper, Nat made his way to the ruined treasury.

He hauled himself up to a window and peered inside …

A bizarre meeting was in progress.

Fellow Cobras, the Head Cobra Lamia has decreed that we will gather in the throne room at sunset tomorrow. At the exact second that the Magnotaur Festival begins, Lamia will blow the Pipes of Paxi and Mount Ophis will awaken!

Once we have demonstrated our control over nature, we will demand that the islanders of Magnos send us, the Cobra gang, one million dollars each year, or else …

The meeting reached its creepy climax.

All hail to Lamia! All power to the Cobra gang!

While the strange crowd trooped out, two familiar figures waited behind.

Lamia's given me this fax with the details of the arrival of the final cobra consignment. All should go smoothly now. Is our bearded friend out of the way, Taki?

Lamia and Smith are taking him to the base as planned, Mr Bogartus. But when I picked him up, I forgot to grab his magazine …

I went back to fetch it and found this! I don't know if the person who wrote it knew about the message in the star feature, but he'd certainly heard about the rendezvous at the hotel.

And then that wretched girl turned up …

First things first. Before the consignment arrives, we must decipher the message and find out where our bearded friend has hidden his information. As for the mystery letter writer, perhaps, with a little persuasion, the girl might tell us who he is. Where is she?

In the chest over there.

Let's get to work on her!

Nat had to distract them, quickly.

The sinister trio raced out.

Someone's watching us from that window. After him!

Nat unbolted the chest. As a dusty figure climbed out, his worst suspicions were confirmed …

Thanks!

He knew what had happened to Al.

What has happened to him?

Magazine Message

Al's assistant, Lina, brushed away a cobweb and gaped at Nat in disbelief as he introduced himself.

Who are you?

I'm Al's cousin, Nat. You must be Lina, his assistant.

"How did you get here?" she asked. "Is Al with you? He arranged to meet me at the Temple of the Magnotaur at midnight. He said he was onto something but he never showed up, and when I went to look for him at Villa Magnotaur, I bumped into that thug called Taki."

September 9

Kaos Today

MOVIE STAR IN SECRET DIG FOR TREASURE

"Old legend of Cobra Gold true!" claims Strega Nimbus.

Spangle City's leading lady turns treasure seeker and excavates ancient site!

Strega in box office smash, Battlestar Elektra.

High-flying twin, Amaretti, boss of Sci Fi Inc

Au revoir! Off to Magnos and the ancient city

Strega,
I've hidden the diary and the photos, as you suggested. In case anything happens, I've concealed the details of their hiding place in the article about the dig in my copy of Kaos Today. Take the letters with dots beneath them and rearrange them to reveal my message.
Al

Strega Nimbus today revealed that she is behind a new excavation of the ruined ancient city of Magnos.

The former movie star claims that her aunt, Elena Nimbus, the archeologist, made vital finds supporting the legend of the Cobra Gold during an earlier excavation of Magnos's Temple of the Magnotaur.

Star mission

"I consider it my duty to continue her work." the glamorous star told a packed press conference. "The treasure must be found and restored to its rightful owners – the islanders of Magnos!"

Her aunt's finds include a frieze depicting the gang of Cobras who, the story goes, held Magnos to ransom; some musical pipes – the so-called Pipes of Paxi – now in Kaos Museum; and two ancient scrolls.

The star claims that one of the scrolls shows a plan of the legendary palace where the Cobras lived, while the other scroll is a letter written in their lost language.

Mystery theft?

Last month, the excavation took an unexpected turn with the discovery of the Cobradiki Stone, an ancient artifact covered with symbols which Strega claimed to match the writing on the so-called Cobra letter. But before the importance of the stone could be established, both it and the scrolls vanished from Strega's safe.

Strange threats

In a further twist, the star confided that strange signs and sinister warnings to keep away from the Cobras had been scrawled on the wall next to the empty safe.

Quickly, Nat told her everything he knew. From what he had heard and seen that night, he was certain that Al had been kidnapped by the strange crowd who called themselves the Cobra gang and smuggled aboard a boat bound for their base. But why?

"Perhaps he found out what those creeps are really up to," Lina suggested. "I can't believe all that baloney about the Pipes of Paxi."

Just then, Nat spotted a note in Al's writing. As he read it, Taki's odd conversation with the character called Mr Bogartus began to make sense.

"Al did have information after all," he said. "And he left Strega Nimbus a coded message in a magazine article revealing its hiding place. Thanks to Taki, the article's here, in front of us."

What does the message say?

The Legend of the Cobra Gold

At the dawn of time, the snake goddess Ophis tricked the gods of Kaos into eating the Apples of Discord. Centuries of strife ensued until the god Paxi played his pipes. Peace was restored and Ophis fell into a deep sleep. The gods imprisoned her in a chamber beneath the earth, reached only by an abyss on the isle of Cobradiki, guarded by 13 mortals called the Cobras.

Paxi gave his pipes to the Head Cobra, Lamia, but with a warning. If Ophis awoke, she must blow down the long pipe but never down the short pipe. Lamia took no heed and as soon as Paxi left, she blew down the short pipe. Ophis awoke and as she shook herself free of her coils, the earth shuddered and the great volcano on the isle of Minos erupted, destroying half the city. Lamia blew down the long pipe and the earth became still as Ophis sank back into sleep.

Lamia declared that the isle of Minos should send the Cobras a shipload of gold each year, or she would awaken Ophis

again. Year after year, the treasury of Minos was emptied. The fearful people scoured their houses for gold and traded whatever they could in return for gold from other lands. Soon they had nothing left.

In desperation, Althea, the ruler of Minos, sought help from the gods of Kaos. The furious gods dispatched their triple-headed hero, the Magnotaur, to Cobradiki. The Magnotaur retrieved Paxi's pipes from Lamia and brought an end to the Cobras' evil threats.

The grateful people of Minos renamed their island Magnos after the hero – but sadly no gold from their years of tribute was ever recovered.

"No good will come of this," said one nervous islander who wished not to be named. "The Cobras should be left alone."

Sister funds amazing new dating machine

The excavation has access to the latest hi-tech equipment, thanks to Strega's twin, Amaretti Nimbus. Her gigantic business empire financed the development at Excelsior Laboratories of a machine capable of dating ancient finds to within a month. Her role in funding this amazing new invention has won

Amaretti the Tycoon of the Year award, due to be presented on September 15 at Kaos City's Grand Hotel. When the ceremony finishes at 9pm, Amaretti plans to sail to Magnos in her luxury yacht, Midas Touch, to collect Strega's latest finds for dating purposes.

"Pipes of Paxi" – used by the Cobras for their sinister schemes?

ne to
gitalis
soon,

Nat

Clifftop Chase

Suddenly an angry shout rang out across the ruined treasury. Nat looked over his shoulder and gulped as he saw Bogartus and his two henchmen, ready to pounce.

"I'll take these," Lina cried, grabbing Bogartus's fax and a carved stone. "Follow me!"

She darted past the villainous trio and sprinted outside. With Bronson's bloodcurdling threats ringing in his ears, Nat hurried after her.

His mind whirled as he ran. What if Bronson and his pals had based themselves on the Cobras in the magazine article? They had stolen the Pipes of Paxi … Could they also be behind the theft from Strega's safe?

Lina raced along the cliff ahead. Then, to Nat's horror, she suddenly disappeared over the edge.

"We've got you," Bronson growled behind him. "You'll regret you ever meddled with the Cobra gang."

Taking a deep breath, Nat swung himself down the rockface. For one long second, he dangled in midair … until his right foot finally hit a ledge.

"Now move your left foot down …"

Nat almost fell off the cliff when he heard Lina's voice in the darkness below. Following her whispered instructions, he inched his way to the bottom. When he stepped onto the shore, he looked up in disbelief at an ornate doorway carved into the rock.

"Welcome to the Temple of the Magnotaur!" Lina smiled. "Sorry about the short cut. Come on in."

Al's information was hidden under the massive altar stone. To move the stone, they had to press Thebe's right eye then Alexi's left eye. Nat stared at a crumbling fresco on the far wall. Were Thebe and Alexi among the bizarre painted figures? Perhaps the strange symbols held the answer.

Can you identify Thebe and Alexi?

Vital Information

Nat and Lina each pressed a painted eye, then watched the altar stone expectantly. For a moment, nothing happened, then, with a low grinding sound, the huge stone slid away to reveal a secret compartment.

Nat eagerly reached inside and fished out Al's diary. Hidden in its pages were some scraps of paper, two photos and a tattered parchment scroll. While Lina examined the scroll, Nat flipped to the last entry in the diary and began to read.

"Look at these," Nat said, passing Lina the photos. "This is proof that Bogartus and Taki were behind the theft from Strega's safe, and …"

He gasped in horror as a massive figure in a billowing white smock loomed in front of them. It was Bronson Colt! How had he got here?

"Hand over that diary," Bronson snarled. "Hurry up! There's no escape this time."

Impatiently, he wrenched the diary from Nat's shaking hands. Then, to Nat's dismay, he ripped it apart, struck a match and set fire to the pages.

"Ha ha, you'll never pin anything on us now," the villain gloated as charred fragments of paper floated up from the flames.

"You've forgotten something!" Lina cried, waving the photos at him. "What about these? And here's half of someone's business card too …"

Bronson dived at her, but she nimbly skipped aside. With a bellow of fury, he tripped into the trench in front of the altar. Quickly Lina ran for the doorway. Bronson shoved Nat aside and charged after her.

"Find Strega!" Lina yelled at Nat. "She lives in the big house on Paxi Square. Explain what's happened. I'll see you later."

Nat dashed outside, blinking in the bright morning light, and began to run along the shore to Magnos Town.

19

The Plot Thickens

At last, Magnos Town came into view. Gasping for breath, Nat raced along the narrow stretch of sand, determined to reach Strega's house and summon help.

As Nat reached the bustling waterfront, a strong smell of fish hit his nostrils. Last night's catch had been unloaded and Magnos's fish market was in full swing.

Nat dodged past swooping seagulls and traders with crates of sardines, and found a sign to Paxi Square.

Minutes later, he stumbled up a steep lane into a large, dusty square. Behind the high railings in front of him stood a grand, but slightly shabby house. Although it was morning, its peeling shutters were still firmly closed.

Nat ran up to the door and tugged the bell pull. A series of bells clanged wildly through the house then there was silence. As he waited, a cold feeling crept down his spine. Had something happened to Strega?

Nat pushed the door gently. To his surprise, it swung open, revealing a long hall.

"Hello there!" he cried. His voice echoed through the house, but there was no answer.

Then he spotted half of a torn business card lying on the marble floor. It looked all too familiar!

When Nat had a closer look, his worst fears were confirmed.

R-R-RING! Nat jumped as the shrill sound of a telephone cut through the silence. He thundered upstairs, dashed across a shadowy room and grabbed the receiver, but the phone went dead.

Nat wrenched open the shutters and the morning sunlight streamed inside. He was in Strega's study.

He picked up an official looking document. As he read its contents, the truth slowly dawned on him. The Cobra legend, the Pipes of Paxi, the bizarre costumes … all these were side issues. Central to the Cobra gang's sinister plot was the safe arrival of the final COBRA consignment.

What is the final consignment?

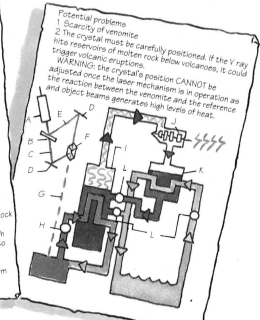

Hood, Wink & Lye

To A.N.
My client needs funds to build the COBRA prototype. We are willing to enter into profit sharing arrangements with any potential backers.

The COBRA (Crystal Originated Beam Reactor)
Inventor : Professor Una Eco
The COBRA will extract limitless supplies of energy from the earth's mantle without any of the disadvantages of conventional means of energy production. It is activated by a simple laser mechanism. The COBRA comprises:

A Laser
B Beam splitter
C Reference beam
D Mirror
E Object beam
F Crystal of venomite - when C and E coincide in the middle of this volatile crystal, they react to form
G The V ray - this creates hot spots in the molten rock comprising the earth's mantle
H Pump to direct hot gases from hot spots through
I Steam generator - steam from hot water rises to
J Turbine - where steam is forced through at high speed to produce electricity
K Condenser - cold water in pipes condenses steam from turbine
L Pumps to direct water around the system

Potential problems
1 Scarcity of venomite
2 The crystal must be carefully positioned. If the V ray hits reservoirs of molten rock below volcanoes, it could trigger volcanic eruptions.
WARNING: the crystal's position CANNOT be adjusted once the laser mechanism is in operation as the reaction between the venomite and the reference and object beams generates high levels of heat.

A Secret Cipher

A s Nat examined the rest of the papers, a dark figure appeared in the doorway … It was Lina.

"We've got to get out of here," she gasped. "That thug in the smock is heading straight for the house!"

The duo raced downstairs only to discover Bronson blocking the front door. Quickly, they turned and fled down the corridor into the garden.

"You'll regret this!" Bronson panted, close behind.

Lina scrambled over the garden wall and landed with a squelch on a crate of grapes in a cart below.

Just as Nat swung himself down, the driver cracked his whip and the cart pulled away. Lina hastily grabbed Nat and hauled him aboard.

"Where's Strega?" she asked as the cart creaked and swayed down the narrow street.

"It looks like the worst has happened," Nat said, producing the torn card. "Somehow, Bogartus and Co. discovered that Strega knew about the COBRA machine."

Nat quickly explained to Lina what the COBRA was. From what he had read in Al's diary, he was convinced that the crooks had built the machine at their base, using components smuggled from Kaos. All they needed now was one vital crystal of venomite.

"Remember the stolen gem called the Serpent's Eye of Enchillada?" he said. "I suspect that it is their final consignment. Once the gem arrives, the gang will activate the machine's laser mechanism and make Mount Ophis erupt, then threaten further eruptions unless Magnos pays up."

"Just like the Cobras in the legend," Lina said. "But what was all that talk about the powers of the Pipes of Paxi at the meeting, and why was …?"

The cart rattled to a halt on the waterfront. Nat and Lina jumped off and dived into a cafe. Munching their way through a pile of sticky pastries, they discussed their next move.

"We've got to intercept the final consignment," Nat said. "It arrives on Magnos today, but we don't know where or when."

"All the details are here, in Bogartus's fax," Lina said, fishing out a torn strip of paper. "There's just one snag – they're in a secret code."

Nat rummaged in his pocket and pulled out a similar strip, together with a grid and a list of words.

"I found these among the papers at Strega's house," he explained.

Nat's strip of paper was covered with meaningless numbers, but unlike Bogartus's fax, someone had added letters which formed a clear message. If they could figure out how the cipher worked, they might be able to decode the secret details of the final consignment's arrival.

What does Bogartus's fax say?

The Final Consignment

Ten minutes later, Nat and Lina waited impatiently on the dock while a port official radioed through to the captain of the Dalliana ferry.

Their hearts sank as the reply crackled through. There was no one called Ophis on the boat. The official shrugged and hurried away as the Dalliana chugged slowly into port.

Nat watched the passengers trickle onto the dock. Two men in dark suits pushed their way through the brightly dressed crowd. Nat instantly recognized the man he had met at the port of Kaos. But who was his sinister sidekick?

The man glanced furtively over his shoulder. He muttered something to his pal and they began to run. Nat raced after them, but it was hopeless. The shady duo leaped aboard a boat which had pulled up by the dock, unnoticed. It was the villains' boat, the Medusa! With a deafening roar, the boat spun around and sped out to sea.

"Ahoy there!" cried Lina. She sat at the helm of a small motorboat and revved the engine impatiently. "It's Al's boat. Jump aboard!"

They trailed the Medusa across the shimmering sea to two rocky islets. Just as the crooks disappeared behind a barren headland, the boat's engine spluttered ominously, shuddered, then went dead.

Lina struggled to restart the motor, but there was not even the faintest spark of life.

"We must have run out of fuel," she groaned. "We'll have to paddle."

The boat tilted precariously as she rummaged for a pair of oars. Soon they were ready to set off.

"Which way?" Lina asked, producing a small chart.

Nat thought hard. The crooks must be heading for their secret base. If the gang had based itself on the legendary Cobras, surely its HQ would be on the island of Cobradiki. But Cobradiki wasn't on Lina's chart ... unless its name had changed.

Where should they go?

Into the Base

Four hot and exhausting hours later, Nat sighted the Medusa at the foot of a steep, forbidding cliff. The blazing sun beat down on them as they rowed over to investigate.

Lina led the way up a flight of steps carved into the rock. Snakes basked in the heat, ignoring her as she carefully crept past.

"So the Cobra part of the legend is true after all," Lina gasped, when she finally reached the top.

Out of a huge crater below rose a vast ancient palace. Golden serpents glittered above its doorways. This had to be the Cobra gang's base.

"We've got to grab the Serpent's Eye before they activate the COBRA machine," Nat said. "According to Bogartus, they're meeting in the throne room at sunset. That must be where they've built the machine … and where we will find the Eye."

Lina pulled out the scroll and the stone that she had picked up earlier. With the help of these objects, they could locate the throne room and figure out which of the entrances below would lead them there.

Where should they enter the palace?

27

Prisoners in the Labyrinth

They were only two rooms away from their goal when Nat raced around a corner and ran straight into Bronson. Then everything went black.

When Nat came to, he breathed in cold, musty air. A dazzling light shone in his eyes. He blinked and saw Lina. Suddenly his watch bleeped six. He jumped to his feet. The Serpent's Eye! They had to find it before the gang activated the COBRA machine.

"There's just one snag," Lina said. "We've been moved. I can't figure out where we are."

She ran down a long, dark passage and turned left into another passage. This led to a flight of steps going down into yet another passage. Nat sprinted after her, not noticing the shadowy figure closing behind him … until it was too late.

Lina turned and looked on in horror, as Nat struggled in the clutches of a huge stranger …

"Nat!" exclaimed a friendly voice. "And Lina too! What are you doing here? What's going on?"

Nat sighed with relief. This was no stranger – it was Al! Al looked dazed as Nat quickly explained what had happened and told him about the Cobra gang's sinister plot.

"And we've got to stop them before it's too late," cried Lina, disappearing up a flight of stairs. "Come on!"

She turned left at the top. Nat and Al followed her down a strange, twisting passage to a dead end.

"Wait!" she gasped, before they could retrace their steps.

On the wall ahead was a painting of a huge maze. With the help of her carved stone, Lina swiftly translated the symbols above it.

"So this is the legendary labyrinth of Ophis," Al said, awestruck. "It was built beneath the Cobras' palace to confuse Ophis if she ever escaped from the abyss … so the story goes."

"And we must be trapped somewhere in the middle," Nat groaned, thinking back to his journey along the darkened passages.

"There's an entrance to the labyrinth from the palace," Lina piped up. "It's marked on the plan with a sign that matches one of the symbols on the painting. It's probably bolted and barred, but it's our only hope."

What is their route to the entrance?

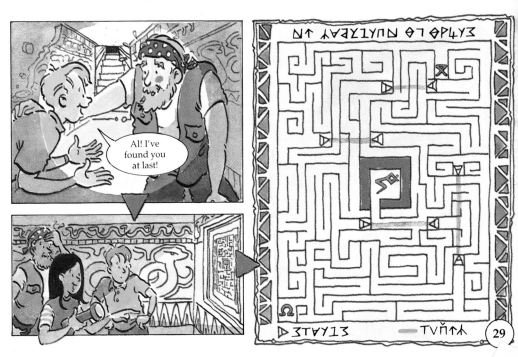

In Search of the COBRA

Luckily for the trio, the trapdoor to the palace was unbolted. Nat, Lina and Al squeezed through the tiny opening and scrambled up into a deserted hall.

"I hope it's not too far to the throne room," Al gulped, looking anxiously at the fading light.

"This way," Lina cried, running over to a grand marble staircase.

As they reached the throne room at the top of the stairs, Nat groaned in despair. They were too late. The gang had already assembled … and there was no sign of the COBRA machine.

None of the bizarrely dressed crooks noticed the horrified trio at the entrance. They were listening intently to a ridiculous masked figure on a podium in front of the throne. It was Bogartus in all his glory.

"Cobras, be vigilant," he declared. "A prisoner is on the loose. But she can't stop us from fulfilling our destiny. By the Pipes of Paxi, Ophis will reawaken and Magnos shall pay us tribute once more!"

What prisoner? Could he mean Strega? Nat saw one tiny glimmer of hope. But where was the COBRA machine? And why weren't all the gangsters at the meeting?

"Watch out," Al hissed, grabbing Nat and Lina. "We've got company."

He dragged them behind a pillar as three more costumed characters swept up the stairway. The leader carried the Pipes of Paxi. Surely this was Lamia, the Head Cobra. Nat instantly recognized her surly attendants.

The three villains paraded into the throne room, then the doors thudded shut and bolts were rammed into place. What could they do now?

"Look at this," Lina gasped, pulling out the ancient plan. "The throne room is twice the size of the room we've just seen and there's a door at each end!"

Why wasn't the COBRA machine in the throne room? Why should the gang want to hide it from view? Nat's mind buzzed with questions as he raced after the others. But when they reached the place where a door was marked on the plan, there was only a painted wall.

"What's happened to the door?" Lina muttered, scratching her head. "It's definitely on the plan."

While Al poked and prodded the wall in search of hidden levers, Nat spotted a panel of buttons to the right.

Buttons! Nat's mind flashed back to a scrap of paper tucked inside Al's diary. It had contained details of a sequence of buttons. If he could remember the sequence, they might find a way inside the hidden room.

Which buttons should Nat press?

Sabotage

As Nat pressed the final button, the wall slid back to reveal an incredible contraption. It had to be the COBRA machine. High up among the fanbelts sparkled a giant crystal.

"The Serpent's Eye!" Nat yelled, charging up a flight of stairs. "We've got to reach it before they start the machine, or it will be too late!"

"Watch out," Al panted behind him. "There's trouble ahead."

Nat looked up and gulped. Two burly figures were lurking at the top. A third man crouched in the shadows by the crystal.

"Not so fast!" Taki growled, brandishing a large spanner.

The next second the two thugs pounced. Nat darted out of their way, ducked under a row of fanbelts and raced over to the crystal. But he had forgotten the third man.

"Grab him, Zither!" cried Taki.

The man sprang at him. Quickly, Nat jumped onto a nearby ladder. As he clambered up past more pulleys and cogs, a plan began to form in his head. Maybe he didn't have to remove the Serpent's Eye after all …

Zither lunged for his ankle, but Nat kicked himself free and staggered up onto a platform. His head swam as he looked down into the throne room far below. He was about to steady himself on a cable when he saw that it was connected to some kind of lever next to the Head Cobra's throne.

Just then, Nat noticed three handles to his right. If he turned just one handle, he could sabotage the gang's fiendish scheme … but what would happen if he chose the wrong one?

"O Ophis awake!" cried a woman's voice, echoing up into the hidden room. "Wreak vengeance on Magnos!"

"You're too late," Zither jeered at Nat, as he scrambled up onto the platform. "You'll never stop us now!"

As a long, shrill note blasted through the air, Nat's brain leaped into action. He had only seconds left to make his vital decision.

Which handle should he turn?

The Palace of Doom

With a gleeful cry, Zither pushed Nat aside and spun all three handles back.

"The laser is still in activation mode," he gloated. "Your feeble sabotage attempt has failed!"

"Not so!" Al panted at the top of the ladder. "As soon as Nat disabled the laser, I grabbed the crystal."

Zither's howls of rage were drowned by an ominous rumbling deep below. Suddenly the whole palace shuddered and foul smelling smoke filled the air. Lina hastily scrambled onto the platform, with Taki and his sinister pal close behind.

BOOM! Everyone dived for cover as a massive explosion ripped through the hidden room.

As twisted machinery flew through the air, Zither and his terrified cronies dashed across the platform, seized the cable attached to the Head Cobra's lever and slithered down into the throne room below.

As another tremor rocked the palace, Nat staggered over to the cable. Luckily it was still firmly secured above ... but for how long?

With chunks of the building raining down on them, the trio abseiled into the throne room. But a figure in a mask was waiting below. Al hung helplessly in midair as Lamia tried to snatch the crystal out of his hand.

"Look out!" cried Lina, as a giant pillar crashed to the ground, narrowly missing the Head Cobra.

Seized by panic, the gangsters raced to the doors, wrenched back the bolts and stampeded outside.

"Flee!" someone shrieked. "It's the revenge of Ophis!"

The villains disappeared through a hole in the palace's outer wall. The next second, the entire wall collapsed in a mountain of rubble.

Not everyone had escaped. By the entrance to the labyrinth, Lina spotted Lamia's hat and the Pipes of Paxi. A fax and an ancient scroll lay nearby.

A familiar sign leaped into focus. In a flash, Lina realized that Lamia knew a safe route out of the doomed palace. The vital details were in front of them. They had to find it – and fast.

What is the safe route?

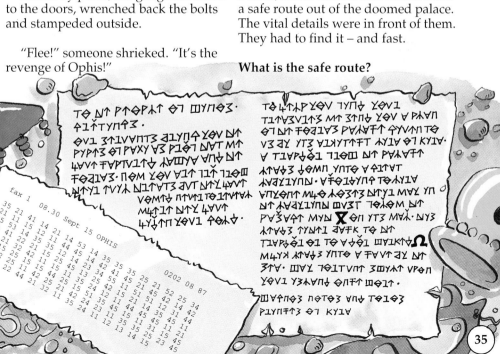

Farewell Cobradiki

Twenty terrifying minutes later, Nat, Lina and Al staggered out of a cave onto the shore. Dark clouds of smoke rolled down the cliff and huge waves smashed against the rocks.

Through the spray, Nat spotted a boat heading out to sea. They frantically tried to attract its attention, but their cries were drowned by a deep roar coming from the very heart of the island.

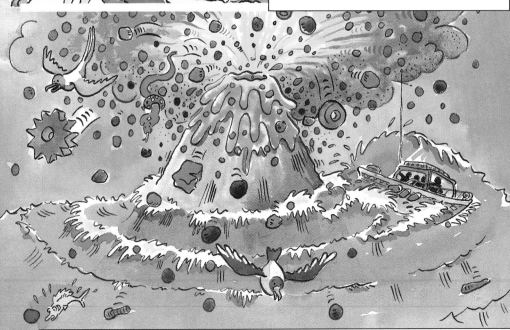

Just as the trio lost hope, the boat turned back. As it approached, Nat's heart sank. It was the Medusa …

"Don't worry!" a cheerful voice cried from the cabin. "Just jump in the back and I'll get us out of here."

They scrambled aboard and sped away from the doomed island.

Suddenly there was a deafening BOOM. A fiery light flashed across the sky, then chunks of molten rock and red hot lava shot through the air.

"So the island was a dormant volcano," said Al. "Its vent must have been directly below the room where the gang built the machine. But why has it erupted now?"

Nat thought hard. Could the laser have triggered the eruption without the Serpent's Eye? Or did the Pipes of Paxi have mysterious powers after all?

"There's someone in the water!" Lina yelled, pointing at a flailing figure in the distance.

The Medusa swiftly turned and headed back across the churning sea. As the boat drew closer, Al threw the stricken stranger a line. She caught it and swam weakly up to the side. Al helped her aboard, while Nat and Lina dashed into the cabin in search of towels and dry clothes.

All they could find were two grubby rags and a half empty bottle of strong Magnotaur liquor. When Nat emerged back on deck, Al was listening sympathetically to the bedraggled stranger's sad tale.

"… and when I returned home, they were waiting for me," she said. "Then everything went black."

"I came to in some kind of labyrinth," the stranger continued. "As I began to search for a way out, the tremors started …"

She clutched at her cloak and shivered. CRASH! Nat dropped the liquor bottle in surprise.

"It's a pack of lies from beginning to end," he cried. "Don't believe a word of it!"

Why not?

The COBRA Project

Strega Nimbus, alias Lamia, sprang to her feet and pointed a pistol at the horrified trio.

"Hands up!" she hissed. "Give me the Serpent's Eye, quickly."

Al reluctantly reached into his pocket and pulled out the crystal. As the last rays of the sun flashed across the gem, Strega paused. She did not notice the figure on the cabin roof, unfurling a large, flapping sail until …

Strega cried out in fury as the heavy sail descended on her, knocking the pistol from her grasp. It fell into the water with a small plop.

"Good riddance!" a cheerful voice cried as the gun disappeared from view.

"Professor Eco!" gasped Nat, glimpsing her face for the first time. "How did you get here?"

"It's a long story," the missing scientist began. "I was looking for funds to build my invention, the COBRA, when I received a letter from someone called Ophis. This person offered to help me if I followed their orders and kept the project secret."

"I believed that my invention would be used to benefit humankind," Eco continued. "So I accepted the proposal. I staged my disappearance and built the COBRA, using parts supplied by Taki."

"I realized that something fishy was going on when Taki brought me the Serpent's Eye," she said. "I made my escape through the labyrinth. I knew which way to go as I had laid pipes through its passages to supply the machine with sea water."

"I found this boat by the cliff," the professor went on. "I met the Magnos fishing fleet when the tremors began. We reached the island in time to pick up Taki and his cronies. They were glad to see us! Now they're on their way to Magnos jail."

Smiling, Eco pointed at a small fleet of boats in the distance. But Nat knew that it was not time to celebrate yet. According to the fax that Lina had found in the Cobras' palace, one big time crook was still at large, known only by the codename, Ophis.

"Look what our friends left behind!" Lina said, popping out of the cabin with a pink notebook. "Perhaps this contains Ophis's true identity."

Nat recognized it instantly. It was the document that he had picked up at the port of Kaos the day before and returned to Zither without ever glancing at its contents.

As Nat read the first pages, everything began to fall into place. At last he knew why Bronson and Niagara had stolen the Pipes of Paxi, and why Bogartus had spun the yarn about their mythical powers.

Most of the gangsters had never known about the COBRA machine. They were just a smokescreen for the operations of a far more sinister outfit.

The pages did not reveal Ophis's name, but Nat had enough to go on. He glanced at his watch. It was 8:30 already. Time was running out …

Who is Ophis?

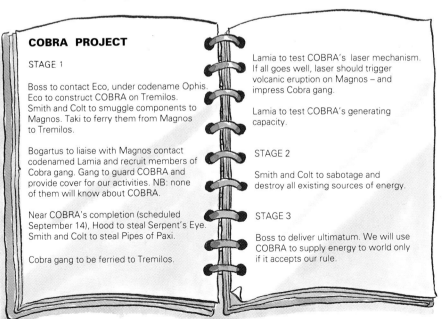

COBRA PROJECT

STAGE 1

Boss to contact Eco, under codename Ophis. Eco to construct COBRA on Tremilos. Smith and Colt to smuggle components to Magnos. Taki to ferry them from Magnos to Tremilos.

Bogartus to liaise with Magnos contact codenamed Lamia and recruit members of Cobra gang. Gang to guard COBRA and provide cover for our activities. NB: none of them will know about COBRA.

Near COBRA's completion (scheduled September 14), Hood to steal Serpent's Eye. Smith and Colt to steal Pipes of Paxi.

Cobra gang to be ferried to Tremilos.

Lamia to test COBRA's laser mechanism. If all goes well, laser should trigger volcanic eruption on Magnos – and impress Cobra gang.

Lamia to test COBRA's generating capacity.

STAGE 2

Smith and Colt to sabotage and destroy all existing sources of energy.

STAGE 3

Boss to deliver ultimatum. We will use COBRA to supply energy to world only if it accepts our rule.

Cobra Gold

BANG! Hundreds of brilliant lights exploded across the dark skies above Magnos.

"The Magnotaur Festival's begun!" Lina whooped. "We've arrived just in time for the firework display."

While Al and Eco moored the boat, Nat and Lina searched the happy dancing crowds for the port official. Strega and the rest of the Cobra gang were safely in the back of a police van, but Ophis was still at large. She was due to leave the port of Kaos any moment now. This sinister crook had to be stopped, before she escaped from the clutches of the law.

"You've got to believe us this time!" Lina insisted, as the official listened to them sceptically. "We'll explain later."

While he radioed through to his colleagues in Kaos, Al and Eco raced down the waterfront carrying two mysterious bundles.

"Long live the Magnotaur!" they cried, plonking two sets of festival horns on Nat's and Lina's heads.

"Although the Magnotaur is obviously a myth," Al added, then ducked hastily as a stray firework whizzed past his left ear.

"Or rather, he was really three people called Magnos, Notos and Toros," he continued. "But the Cobra Gold must be a legend. No one's ever found a trace of it …"

"Strega did," Lina said. "She discovered that the ancient Cobras stored the gold in the secret chamber behind the throne room."

"What happened to it?" asked Eco, puzzled. "I never saw any gold there when I was building the COBRA."

"I know where it is," Nat grinned.

Where is the Cobra Gold?

KAOTIC TIMES

STAR IN COBRA CONSPIRACY

SU SPURIOS, Chief Reporter

STREGA NIMBUS, star of "Battlestar Elektra", played a leading role in the Cobra conspiracy, it emerged yesterday.

There was uproar in the courtroom when Strega Nimbus was unmasked as the leader of the Cobra gang. This organization aimed to extort vast sums of money from the island of Magnos. Its members included top executives from the Hudlum City company, Sci Fi Inc, and the notorious gangsters, Niagara Smith and Bronson Colt.

STAR TURNS LOOTER

Ms. Nimbus was also charged with looting the treasures of Magnos, the so-called Cobra Gold, from the island of Tremilos. It was alleged that she plotted to sell the treasures through a firm of Hudlum City art dealers.

How the Cobra gang intended to force Magnos into handing over its millions remains a mystery. Speculation has been fueled by the trial of a person identified only as X. The press were not admitted to the proceedings which were held in conditions of top secrecy.

Villa Magnotaur
Magnotaur Passage
Town Wall
Magnos Town

Dear Nat,

Here are the photos I promised you, together with some newspaper clippings. I hope they make interesting reading! Notice there's no mention of a certain machine. It's all been hushed up.

I've just received a letter from Eco. She's returned the Serpent's Eye to the Geological Society of Enchillada. The Enchilladans are very grateful and they've invited you, me and Lina over to Enchillada next month to be presented with a small reward.

Meanwhile Lina and I are still busily assessing the Cobra Gold With the help of the new dating machine at Excelsior Laboratories, we've discovered that some of the treasures are 3,999 years old! And you'd never guess, a team of Enchilladan geologists has just found evidence of a volcanic eruption on Magnos exactly 4,000 years ago. No wonder the poor islanders paid up!

See you soon,

Al

MYSTERY DISAPPEARANCE OF TYCOON OF THE YEAR

AMARETTI NIMBUS of Sci Fi Inc vanished in mysterious circumstances after receiving the TYCOON OF THE YEAR award at Kaos City's Grand Hotel.

The SFI boss won the award for funding Excelsior Laboratories' hi-tech dating machine. She was last seen speeding off to the port of Kaos in her limousine.

Amaretti with award

STOLEN PIPES RETURN TO MUSEUM

Leading archeologist Al Rose and his assistant Lina Rebus present the Pipes of Paxi to Professor Kurios, curator of Kaos Museum. The priceless pipes were stolen last month by Niagara Smith and Bronson Colt of the Cobra gang. Latest developments in the Cobra conspiracy trial on p.3.

Clues

Answers

Pages 4-5

The Morse signal is not in another code. It has just been sent in reverse order. With the missing letters added, it says:

MEDUSA – RENDEZVOUS AT MAGNOS OLD PORT AT 01:11 AS PREVIOUSLY ARRANGED – LAMIA

Pages 6-7

First, Nat has to locate Villa Magnotaur by recalling his own route there. The villa is up a short passage across a street, opposite the steps to the top of the town wall (see page 6). There are two places on the map which match this location. Nat can figure out which is the correct location by following Taki's directions from Styx Street to the villa in reverse order. Now he can trace Taki's route from Villa Magnotaur to Hotel Digitalis, via Hotel Hydra. This is marked in black. Nat's short cut is shown in red.

Hotel Digitalis   Styx Street

Hotel Hydra   Villa Magnotaur

Pages 8-9

It looks like the strange duo are the notorious gangsters and masters of disguise, Niagara Smith and Bronson Colt.

When Nat spots the duo by the truck outside Hotel Digitalis, one of them (a woman) is wearing a red S shaped earring, but in the next picture it is missing. This must be the red snake earring that Nat finds in the truck. An identical earring was mentioned on the 6:30 news (page 3). Its discovery after a theft from Kaos Museum led police to link the crime with Smith and Colt.

Then there are the instructions on the typed note (page 7), "Rendezvous with S and C at 01:11 at Hotel Digitalis". Could S and C be Smith and Colt?

Finally, the cloaked woman addressed someone outside the hotel as "Bron". Could this be short for Bronson Colt?

Pages 10-11

According to the handwritten message on the scrap of paper, there is a meeting at the Treasury. This must be where Bronson is going. The scrap is from a guide book and it reveals that the Treasury is in the East Quarter of the ancient city of Magnos. When you compare the plan on the scrap of paper with the view from the balcony, you will see that the Treasury must be one of the ruins below.

(continued)

Pages 10-11 (continued)

If you match up the plan with the ruins, you can locate the Treasury by a process of elimination. According to the scrap of paper, the Treasury was not built by Spurios, Vikarios or Notalos, or by Prekarios, who built the Temple of Paxi, so it must have been built by Tritos. The Treasury cannot be B, which is the Ampitheater, or C, which was built by Spurios, or E, which was wrongly attributed to Tritos. This means that it must be A or D.

Before you can find out which one is the Treasury, you have to identify E and C. The Ampitheater (B) was not built by Tritos, Spurios, Prekarios or Vikarios, so its builder must be Notalos. E was not

This is the Treasury.

built by Tritos, Vikarios or Spurios, and now you know it was not built by Notalos, so its builder must be Prekarios and it must be the Temple of Paxi. The Gymnasium is not A, B or D, and it cannot be E, so it must be C.

The House of Althea is not D, and it cannot be B, C or E. This means that it must be A and the Treasury must be D.

Pages 12-13

Al must have been kidnapped by Taki and taken to the Cobra gang's base. All the evidence points this way.

At the bizarre meeting, the man in the mask called Mr. Bogartus is talking about "our bearded friend". Think back to Al's photo (page 3). Could this person be Al?

The note that Taki found when he returned to the mystery person's house looks familiar. It is the note that Nat left under Al's door on page 8. It looks like Taki picked up the "bearded friend" from Villa Magnotaur.

When the girl who bumped into Taki after he found Nat's note turns out to be Al's assistant, Lina, it is obvious that Taki was at Villa Magnotaur.

This all fits in with Taki's movements before the meeting. Remember his instructions on the typed note (page 7) and the cloaked woman's orders (page 8). Could Al have been his "cargo"?

Pages 14-15

The letters with dots below them form this message:

OGTOELPMETOFRUATONGAMANDSSER
PTHEBESTHGIREYENEHTALEXISTFELE
YEOTMOVERATLASTONEDNAFINDNOIT
AMROFNI

Starting with the first word, every alternate word has been written in reverse. Decoded, the message says:

GO TO TEMPLE OF MAGNOTAUR AND
PRESS THEBE'S RIGHT EYE THEN
ALEXI'S LEFT EYE TO MOVE ALTAR
STONE AND FIND INFORMATION

Pages 16-17

Thinking back to the legend of the Cobra Gold (page 15), the three headed man in the fresco must be the Magnotaur. In the right hand painting, there are nine symbols above his neck. Could these spell "Magnotaur" in an ancient script? Except for G, N and U, the symbols are similar to their corresponding letters in the modern alphabet. Using "Magnotaur" as a key, together with your knowledge of the legend, you can translate the symbols above the other people in the right hand painting as "Lamia and the Cobras" and the symbols below the musical pipes as "the Pipes of Paxi". Now you can decode most of the symbols on the fresco and deduce what the remaining symbols must be. This is what they say:

IN FRONT OF PRINCE NIOBE AND PRINCESS THEBE, ALTHEA OF MINOS VOWS TO PROTECT THE PIPES OF PAXI AND USE THEM ONLY IF OPHIS SHOULD AWAKEN AGAIN.

AT THE PALACE OF THE GODS ON THE ISLE OF KIRA DUE EAST OF COBRADIKI, PAXI SENTENCES LAMIA TO BE SET ADRIFT ON THE ICY SEAS OF MISEROS FOR ETERNITY.

THE MAGNOTAUR GIVES A LETTER TO ANATO, A SCROLL TO ALINA AND THE PIPES OF PAXI TO ALEXI, AND ORDERS HIS SERVANTS TO SAIL TO MINOS, SOUTH WEST OF COBRADIKI.

LAMIA GLARES AT THE MAGNOTAUR IN DEFIANCE. NOW SHE HAS LOST ALL HER POWERS, BUT SHE VOWS THAT SHE WILL NEVER REVEAL WHERE THE TREASURES OF MINOS LIE HIDDEN.

ALTHEA   THE SERVANTS OF THE MAGNOTAUR

This is Thebe.   This is Alexi.

Pages 20-21

Reading the document, the strange conversation that Al recorded in his diary (page 18) begins to make sense. The Cobra gang have built a machine called the COBRA (Crystal Operated Beam Reactor) and plan to use it to trigger a volcanic eruption on Magnos on Saturday. All they are waiting for is the arrival of the final COBRA consignment. At the port of Kaos (page 4), the man in the suit told Niagara and Bronson that this consignment had been held up in Enchillada. According to Al's diary, the Enchilladan consignment is a crystal. One of the COBRA's vital components happens to be a crystal of venomite. Remember the news clipping in Al's villa (page 7)? It contains an item about a stolen venomite crystal called the Serpent's Eye of Enchillada. This must be the final consignment.

Pages 22-23

The word SNAKE appears at the top of the decoded fax and along the top row of the grid on the square piece of paper, with the remaining letters of the alphabet written below. The first letter of the fax, L, has been encoded by taking the number 3 from the beginning of its row on the grid, followed by the number 4 from the top of its column. The rest of the fax has been encoded using the same principle.

As COBRA is typed at the top of Bogartus's fax, you have to draw a new grid to decode it, based on the original grid, but with COBRA written along the top row. Decoded, the fax says:

LAMIA – EYE TO ARRIVE ON DALLIANA FERRY TOMORROW MORNING AT NINE – OPHIS

Pages 24-25

According to the writing on the fresco (see pages 16-17), the island of Minos lies south west of Cobradiki and the island of Kira lies due east. Kira is on the chart, but there is no sign of Minos. If you flip back to the magazine article on page 15, you will see that Minos was the ancient name of Magnos. The only island on the chart which has Magnos to its south west and Kira to its east is Tremilos. This must be Cobradiki's modern name and this is where Nat and Lina should go.

Pages 26-27

On the stone, there are two kinds of symbols arranged in alternate rows. One is similar to the writing on the fresco (pages 16-17), while the other is similar to the writing on the scroll. Look at the third row of symbols. Could it be a translation of the second row? Thinking back to the fresco, you know what the symbols in the third row are in the modern alphabet, so you can figure out what the symbols above them must be.

Now you can decipher the contents of the scroll and locate the Throne Room. To get there Nat and Lina should enter the door in the top left hand corner and follow the route marked in black. The rooms that they must go through are numbered in order.

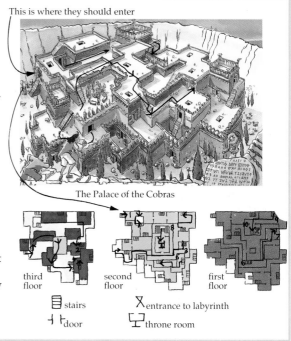

This is where they should enter

The Palace of the Cobras

third floor

second floor

first floor

🗄 stairs   𝗫 entrance to labyrinth

🚪 door   🎏 throne room

Pages 28-29

First, you have to figure out where the trio are. After they came to, Nat and Lina ran along a passage to a junction, turned left, then ran down a flight of steps into another passage where they met Al. At the end of this passage, they ran up more steps, then turned left and followed a winding passage around to a dead end. There is only one route they could have taken. It leads here.
On the plan of the palace (see the answer above), the symbol 𝗫 marks the entrance to the labyrinth. This symbol is on the plan of the labyrinth and this is where they should go. The route is shown in black.

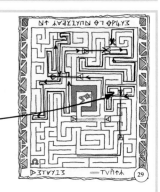

Pages 30-31

The white scrap of paper on page 18 is the key to the sequence. You have to press five buttons to enter the secret chamber. The third button is two buttons above the first and it isn't in the top row, so it must be in the second row. The fourth button must be in the first or second row as the second button is two buttons below it. The third and the fourth buttons have the same symbol. Looking at the panel, this has to be a snake or a triangle. The fifth button is next to the fourth. If the symbol on the fourth is a triangle, then the symbol on the fifth must be a snake. But the fifth has the same symbol as the first and the second, and the buttons which occupy the two possible positions of the first button have circles. This means that the third and the fourth buttons must have snakes and the fourth is in the top row. Now it is easy to locate the first, second and fifth buttons. The sequence is shown above.

Pages 32-33

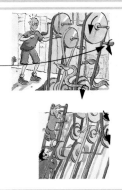
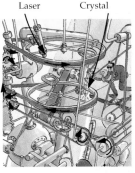

Laser   Crystal

Nat can sabotage the gang's plot by turning this handle which is connected to the wheel with the laser and the wheel with the crystal. This will make it impossible for the COBRA to create the deadly V ray (see the diagram on page 21). The arrows show what will happen.

Pages 34-35

The fax is decoded using the method described in the answer for pages 22-23. Its keyword is OPHIS. It says:

LAMIA - I WILL LEAVE KAOS PORT IN M.T. AT NINE. WILL PICK YOU UP FROM BASE THEN SAIL TO MAGNOS OLD PORT TO ASSESS RESULTS OF STAGE ONE AND COLLECT COBRA GOLD.
OPHIS

This doesn't help now, but it could prove useful later on. Maybe the scroll's contents could be more helpful. The wrriting on the scroll is similar to that on the stone and the plan of the Cobras' palace (pages 26-27). Translated into the modern alphabet, it says:

TO THE PEOPLE OF MINOS, GREETINGS
OUR SERVANTS BRING YOU THE PIPES OF PAXI AS PROOF THAT WE HAVE CAPTURED LAMIA AND THE COBRAS. NOW YOU ARE FREE FROM THEIR EVIL THREATS BUT THEY HAVE VOWED NEVER TO REVEAL WHERE THEY HAVE HIDDEN YOUR GOLD.
TO HELP YOU FIND YOUR TREASURES, WE SEND YOU A PLAN OF THE COBRAS' PALACE, GIVEN TO US BY ITS ARCHITECT, LIRA OF KIRA. A TRAP DOOR FROM THE PALACE LEADS DOWN INTO A GREAT LABYRINTH. ACCORDING TO LIRA, ANYONE WHO LOSES THEIR WAY IN THE LABYRINTH MUST FOLLOW THE PASSAGE WITH ▽ ON ITS WALL. THIS LEADS EITHER BACK TO THE TRAPDOOR OR TO A DOOR MARKED ♎ WHICH LEADS INTO A CAVE BY THE SEA.
MAY FORTUNE SMILE UPON YOUR ISLAND ONCE MORE.
MAGNOS, NOTOS AND TOROS, PRINCES OF KIRA

(continued)

Pages 34-35 (continued)

Now it is obvious that there is a way out of the palace through the labyrinth. The route is shown in black.

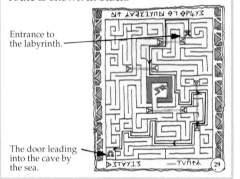

Entrance to the labyrinth.

The door leading into the cave by the sea.

Pages 36-37

The stranger is Al's boss, Strega Nimbus, alias Lamia, the Head Cobra. The telltale sign is the scar on her right arm. Now Nat knows why Strega refused to contact the police, how Al's note about the magazine message fell into the hands of the Cobra gang and who the cloaked woman at Magnos Old Port really was.

Pages 38-39

Ophis is Strega's twin sister, Amaretti Nimbus. This fits in with the contents of the fax on page 35. It was sent on September 15 – the same day that Amaretti was to be in Kaos, according to the magazine (page 15). Both Amaretti and Ophis are planning to leave Kaos at 9pm. Amaretti will set sail in her luxury yacht, Midas Touch. Could this be the "M.T." mentioned in the fax?

Along the way, you may have noticed that the fax number on the torn SFI business

fax 1   08.30 Sept 15 OPHIS   0202 08 87

card (see pages 18 and 20) matches the number on Ophis's faxes. According to the magazine, Amaretti is the boss of Sci Fi Inc (SFI).

Did you read the note to A.N. (page 21), seeking funds for the COBRA? Remember that Amaretti funds inventions. Could the note have been the starting point for the COBRA project?

Page 40

According to the fax on page 35, Ophis and Lamia were planning to collect the Cobra Gold from Magnos Old Port. Thinking back to the white scrap of paper in Al's diary (page 18), someone has removed gold from the hidden room in the Cobras' palace and taken it to the cellar of Hotel Digitalis... which is at Magnos Old Port! That must be the final resting place of the legendary Cobra Gold.

First published in 1995 by Usborne Publishing Ltd, Usborne House, 83-85 Saffron Hill, London EC1N 8RT, England. Copyright © 1995 Usborne Publishing Ltd.

The name Usborne and the device 🐝 are Trade Marks of Usborne Publishing Ltd. All rights reserved.

Printed in Portugal   UE
First published in America August 1995.